SMELL THE DAISIES

"Sally Mander.
Where are you?"

To the Sprinklers: Isaac, Leni, Eleanor, Reis, and Yasemin, too, who is a sprinkler of sorts — J.H.

For my cousins — T.L.M.

Text © 2019 Judith Henderson
Illustrations © 2019 Trenton McBeath

Kids Can Press gratefully acknowledges the financial support of the Government of Ontario, through Ontario Creates; the Ontario Arts Council; the Canada Council for the Arts; and the Government of Canada for our publishing activity.

Published in Canada and the U.S. by Kids Can Press Ltd.
25 Dockside Drive, Toronto, ON M5A 0B5

Kids Can Press is a Corus Entertainment Inc. company

www.kidscanpress.com

The artwork in this book was rendered in graphite pencil and colored in Photoshop.
The text is set in Bizzle-Chizzle.

Edited by Yasemin Uçar
Designed by Julia Naimska and Andrew Dupuis

Printed and bound in Malaysia in 3/2019 by Tien Wah Press (Pte) Ltd.

CM 19 0 9 8 7 6 5 4 3 2 1

Library and Archives Canada Cataloguing in Publication

Henderson, Judith, author
    Smell the daisies / written by Judith Henderson ; illustrated by T. L. McBeth.

(Big words small stories ; 3)
Short stories.
ISBN 978-1-77138-790-3 (hardcover)

    1. Readers (Elementary). I. McBeth, T. L., illustrator II. Title.

PE1117.H46145 2019   428.6'2   C2018-906085-9

BIG WORDS
small stories

SMELL THE DAISIES

"AHA!"

THWAT!

Written by Judith Henderson

Illustrated by T. L. McBeth

KIDS CAN PRESS

Table of Contents

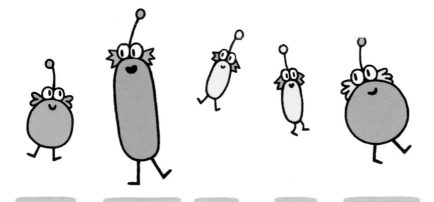

Who's Who

Meet Oleander (that's O-lee-an-durr). She likes to keep busy.

Meet Sally Mander. She prefers to take it easy.

Meet the Sprinkle Fairy.

She has a word factory in Sicily. That's where the best words in the world come from.

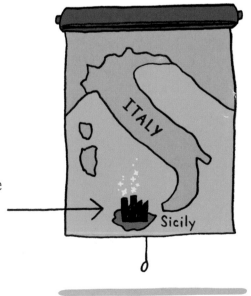

These are the Sprinklers. They're the Sprinkle Fairy's helpers.

They sprinkle Big Words into small places. If you happen to spot a Sprinkler in a story, it means there's a Big Word coming!

BIG WORD!

"The finest words — fresh from the factory!"

The Early Bird
and the Worm

"Let's go out for breakfast today."

THWAT!

"I prefer to let my breakfast come to me."

THWAT!
THWAT!
THWAT!

"Come on, you need the exercise."

Sigh

"Okay, okay."

10

"See? It's a lovely day."

"Ooh! A fat, juicy ..."

"Worm!"

"Hey! That's my worm!"

"No, it's *my* worm!"

"It's mine!"

"I'm nobody's worm!!!"

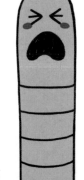

11

"Stop! Everybody step away from the worm!"

"What is going on? I could hear you guys all the way over in Sicily!"

"And Sicily is really far, by the way."

"This is my worm! I saw it first."

"So? I saw it second."

GULP!

"Yum. All gone."

"Big Word coming. BIG!"

"Bird, regurgitate that worm right now!"

"REGURGITATE!
Big Word! Big Word!"

Say it: ree-GUR-jih-tayt

"I shall **NOT** regurgitate that which I ate."

"I suggest that you regurgitate before it's too late."

"Or what?"

"Or I'll turn you into a hot dog."

"A hot dog?"

"It's something people eat, with mustard and relish."

"*And* onions."

"Oh, well, in that case ..."

BURRRRP!

"I'm freeeee!"

"Nobody's getting the worm today."

"And now it's too late for breakfast."

"I told you we should have stayed home."

BURRRRP!

REGURGITATE is a Big Word
that means to burp up something
that was swallowed.

No Bare Feet

-Daily Special-
French Flies

"Ooh, my favorite — grilled cheese sandwich with tomato soup."

"And they have french flies!"

"Oh, there's the Sprinkle Fairy. Hi, Sprinkle Fairy!"

"You have got to try these meatballs. They are divine."

"Excuse me, is the salamander with you?"

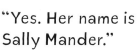

"Big Word coming. BIG!"

"Yes. Her name is Sally Mander."

"Sally Mander, you will have to leave."

"Leave? WHY?"

"Because Sally Mander is not wearing the proper attire."

"ATTIRE!
Big Word! Big Word!"

Say it: uh-TY-urr

"ATTIRE — as in, clothes. See the sign?"

"I don't need a tire. I'm wearing a tutu."

PROPER ATTIRE
No bare feet.
No bare anything!

"Everyone else is wearing proper attire."

"Come on, Sally Mander.
We're leaving."

"But I really want
french flies."

"Well ... then
we'll have to
get you some
clothes."

"Let's start with
some shoes."

"Hi, Mr Footz, we're
looking for shoes for
Sally Mander."

"I have one pair left in your size."

"I love them!"

"Sprinkle Fairy! Look — I got new sandals."

"You're going to need more than sandals for the diner. Hmm. Let's see ..."

POOF! POOF! POOF!

"All ready!"

"Are you sure?"

"Yup."

"I don't think that's proper attire."

"No bare feet. No bare anything. And a tire. Now — I'll have a double order of french flies, please."

ATTIRE is a Big Word
that means clothes.

Stronger by the Minute

"Hi, Sprinkle Fairy. I see you are exercising."

"I'm building strong muscles."

"I don't need to exercise. Look at my muscles."

DINK!

"Not bad, but look at these."

DA-  DONK!

"Wow. How do I get those?"

"You can borrow my weights. They work like magic."

Wink!

POOF!

"Look at me!"

"Oleander, hand me that big weight."

"Maybe you should start with something more your size."

"Yeah, more your size. Heh heh."

"Easy peasy."

"Oh, yeah?"

"Light as a feather."

"Light as no feathers!"

"Get a load of this!"

GASP!

"Big Word coming! BIG!"

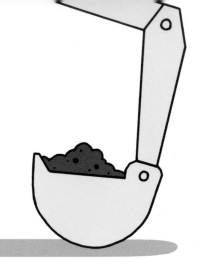

"Sally Mander, I am *flabbergasted!*"

"FLABBERGASTED!
Big Word! Big Word!"

"I sure
showed him."

"TA-DA! Fishing, anyone?"

"Oh, yeah? How about this WHALE of a weight!"

"You're scaring the whale! Give me back my weights."

"That was flabbergasting, Sally Mander."

"Yes, I even amazed myself."

"Need a lift?"

FLABBERGASTED is a Big Word
that means to be very surprised and
amazed by something.

Smell the Daisies

"It's time to plant the daisies, Sally Mander."

"Oh, good. I love watching you plant daisies."

"No, WE are going to plant the daisies. Here's your shovel."

"You start here. I'll start there. We'll finish at the fence."

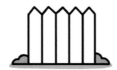

Hello, little daisy. Are you happy now in the warm, soft, earthy ground?"

"Sixty-four daisies ..."

"Daisy Number Two,
meet Daisy Number One."

"Seventy-eight ...
seventy-nine daisies ..."

"Hi, Sally Mander.
Nice day for
planting daisies."

"Yes, I've already
planted two."

"Looks like you have a lot more to go."

"That's why I'm going to have a rest now."

"I've got just the thing."

POOF!

"Ta-da! A picnic. Care for a worm sandwich?"

"Yes, please!"

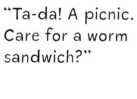

"That's one hundred and six daisies."

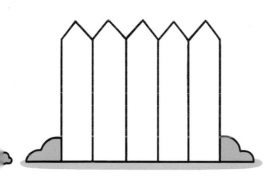

"Sally Mander?"

"There you are! What are you doing?!"

"We're taking time to smell the daisies."

"Sally Mander ..."

"Big Word coming!
BIG!"

"You're procrastinating."

"PROCRASTINATING!
Big Word! Big Word!"

Say it: pro-KRAS-tin-ayt-ing

"You only planted two daisies!"

"So?"

"So, it's time to get back to work."

"No more worm sandwiches for you, Sally Mander."

"Planting daisies is no picnic."

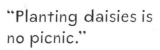

PROCRASTINATING is a Big Word that means putting off doing something that should be done.

Time for Tea

"Big news,
Sally Mander!
The Queen has
invited us for
tea today!"

"Woo-hoo! I'm
going to find
something
fancy to wear."

"Hurry up, Sally
Mander! The taxi
is here!"

"Remember to
mind your manners
when you're with
the Queen."

"Okay, okay."

"Wow!"

"We're having tea
with the Queen.

"Quite."

"The Queen
will see you in
the garden."

"Welcome.
You're just
in time."

"The Sprinkle Fairy was just sharing her secret hot dog recipe."

"Oh, yes. The Sprinkle Fairy is famous for her hot dogs."

THWAT!

"Sally Mander!"

"But they have good bugs here."

"Excuse me, your majesty ... Sally Mander, mind your manners!"

"Big Word coming. BIG!"

"Not to worry, my dear. It was just a peccadillo."

"PECCADILLO!
Big Word! Big Word!"

"Sally Mander, we made these bug-and-wormy biscuits just for you."

"Don't mind if I do."

"Mmmm. The Pickle-dillo gives it a nice crunch."

Say it: peck-ah-**DILL**-o

PECCADILLO is a Big Word
that means a small mistake.

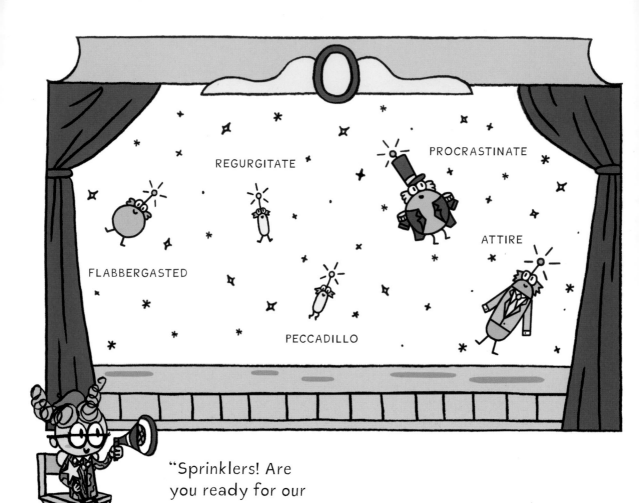

REGURGITATE

PROCRASTINATE

FLABBERGASTED

ATTIRE

PECCADILLO

"Sprinklers! Are you ready for our Small Play on Big Words?"

"Ready!"

"Lights! Camera! Action!"

"Ladies and gentlemen, boys and girls! Do not drag your feet. Do not PROCRASTINATE."

"Come and behold the Great Burper, who will gobble a worm and then REGURGITATE it!"

"The Great Burper regurgitates the worm a magnificent distance! You will be FLABBERGASTED!"

BURRRRP!

Sigh

OOOOOOH-AHHHHHH!

"How rude! The worm has landed
on my fancy ATTIRE."

SPLAT!

"Don't yell at the worm. It was
just a PECCADILLO."

"Yes, please don't
yell at me. It's been
a long day."

Also available in the
Big Words Small Stories series:

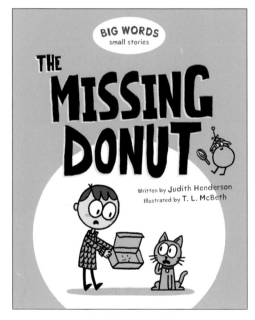

978-1-77138-788-0

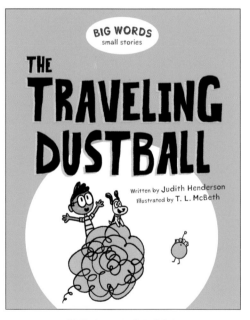

978-1-77138-789-7

"A HUMDINGER for budding wordplay fans."
— *Booklist*